To My Mom
You are the true Oh So Fancy Nana!
Thank you for always believing in me and
encouraging me to go for it!

Stay fancy Nana!! I Love You!

ISBN-13: 978-1477628737 ISBN-10: 1477628738

Visit us at www.maggiesuebooks.com
JennLynn Creative Management

My Oh So Fancy Nana!

By Maggie Pearson

Illustrations by Reginald L Weatherspoon

This is my Nana..

She is SO fancy!!

My Nana has a fancy house,
and fancy clothes.
My Nana has a fancy dog.
She even has fancy toes!

My Nana eats fancy bread,
with fancy kinds of cheese.

Shes likes for my brother and I to say, "yes ma'am" and "please."

My Nana drives a fancy car.

Her car is always clean and white.

My Nana wears fancy glasses,
all sparkly with jewels
in colors that are bright.

My Nana has lots of fancy friends.
She plays lots of games with them...
like golf, tennis, mahjong and gin.

My Nana has four (not fancy) grandkids.
She says we are a handful.

My Nana laughs a lot with us.

She says, "You kids make life fanciful!"

My Nana buys us fancy toys.
She likes for us to share.

She says that fancy kids
grow up to love and care.

When I grow up, she says, "Darling, you'll be just as fancy as me!"

21667611R00017

Made in the USA
San Bernardino, CA
31 May 2015